DISNEY PRINCESS

Dreams Come True

pi
kids ®

An imprint of PHOENIX International Publications, Inc.

Chicago • London • New York • Hamburg • Mexico City • Sydney

MW01094826

Tonight, floating lanterns will fill the sky with light, and, for the first time, Rapunzel will be a part of it. Her lifelong dream is about to come true! Inside a village shop, Rapunzel feasts her eyes on lanterns of all shapes and sizes.

Before the sun sets, find these lovely lights:

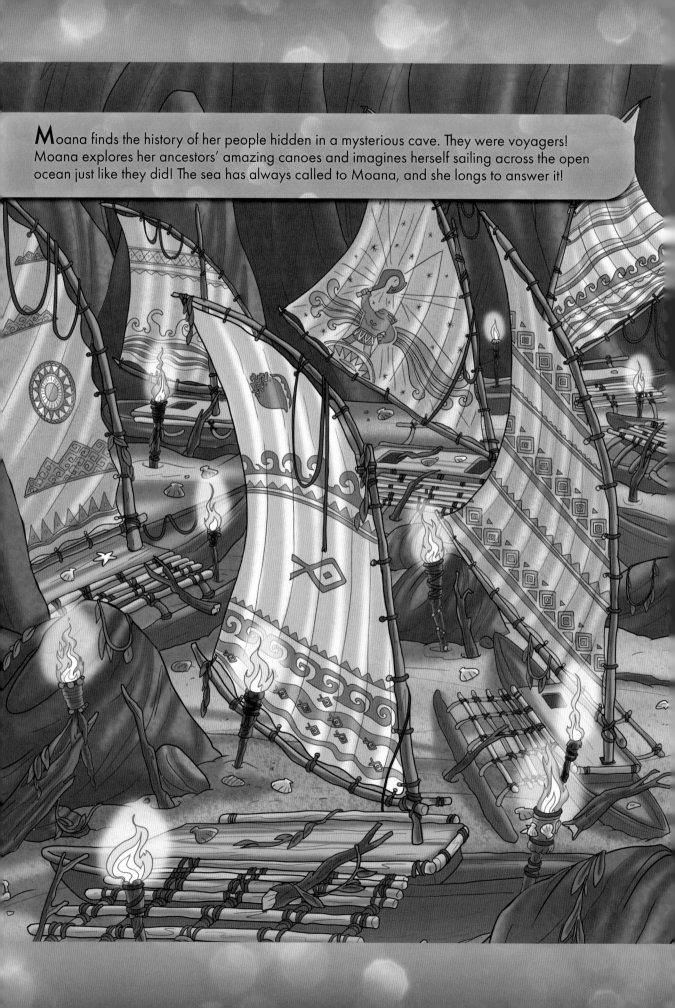

Moana finds the history of her people hidden in a mysterious cave. They were voyagers! Moana explores her ancestors' amazing canoes and imagines herself sailing across the open ocean just like they did! The sea has always called to Moana, and she longs to answer it!

Inspect the canoes in the cave to find these images on their sails:

double spiral   sea turtle   island   Maui   sun   dolphin   school of fish

Tiana has always dreamed of opening a restaurant, and now that dream has come true! People visit from all over to taste Tiana's world-famous gumbo and dance to lively jazz music. And Tiana's family and friends support her through it all!

Grand Opening

Look around for these things every great restaurant should have:

lucky horseshoe

newspaper review

banner

reservation book

menu

opening-day photo

signature dish

Jasmine loves to learn about the world outside of the palace walls. There is so much to see and explore! Someday, Jasmine hopes to go on adventures that will take her to all of the interesting places she has read about.

Look around for these glimpses of the world beyond the palace:

windmill
drawing

bonsai tree

waterfall

conch shell

snowy
mountain

book
of animals

mbira

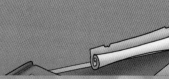

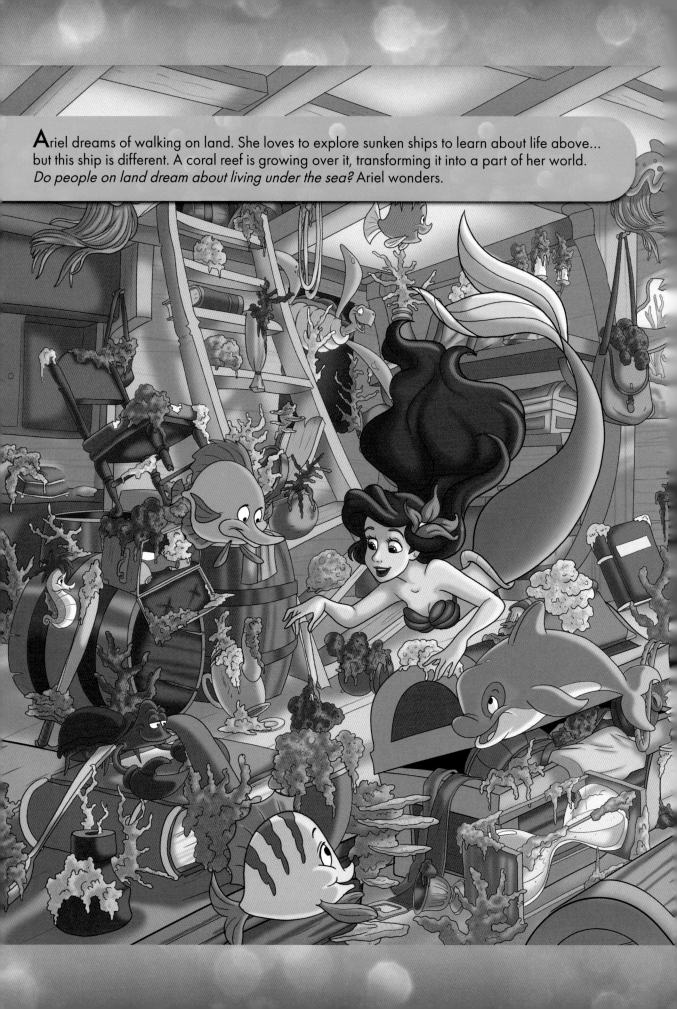

Ariel dreams of walking on land. She loves to explore sunken ships to learn about life above... but this ship is different. A coral reef is growing over it, transforming it into a part of her world. *Do people on land dream about living under the sea?* Ariel wonders.

Float around and find Ariel's under-the-sea neighbors:

turtle   seahorse   dolphin   shrimp   shark   nautilus   ray   crab

Mulan practices her calligraphy every day. She also practices sword fighting, archery, martial arts, horseback riding, and strategizing! Mulan knows that all of these skills are useful and will help her be the person that her family raised her to be.

As Mushu tries to help, search around for these important implements:

saddle staff rope map brush sword arrow apple

Cinderella waltzes across the dance floor, enjoying the music and the company at her royal ball. She wants all the guests to enjoy themselves, so she has made special accommodations for the tiniest of her friends. It just wouldn't be a ball without them!

ROYAL MOUSE BALL

While the dancers count their steps, look for Cinderella's animal companions:

Jaq

Luke

Mary

Suzy

Bert

Gus

Perla

Mert

Belle spends hours in the castle library dreaming and reading about adventures and far-off places. But today, Belle is choosing books to donate to the village library. She wants everyone to have the chance to look through these windows to the world!

While Belle and her friends pick out books, look around the library for these worldly stories:

Float back to the lantern shop and find 20 suns that are as golden as Rapunzel's magical hair.

Sail back to Moana's cave to discover these glowing torches:

Jump back to Tiana's restaurant to find these hard workers:

Go back to Jasmine's room to look for these animals that she hopes to see in the wild:

zebra

flamingo

giraffe

bear

rhino

lion

elephant

Swim back to the sunken ship with Ariel and find these objects transformed by the reef:

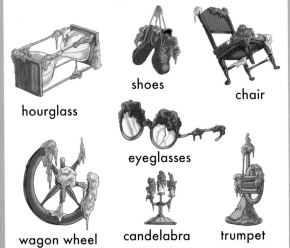

hourglass

shoes

chair

eyeglasses

wagon wheel

candelabra

trumpet

Just like people, flowers are unique. Ride back to Mulan's practice and spot these one-of-a-kind magnolia blossoms.

Dance back to the ball and find these tiny touches Cinderella made for her furry friends:

cheese plate

chair

ice sculpture

ROYAL MOUSE BALL

banner

punch bowl

candle

bouquet

There are more than just books in the castle library! Page back to Belle's book donation and look for these amazing artworks:

stone bust

cuckoo clock

woven rug

suit of armor

watercolor painting

lion statue

ink drawing